Caleb Takes a Ride on the Staten Island Ferry

Written by Catherine Avery St. Jean
Illustrated by Paul J. Frahm

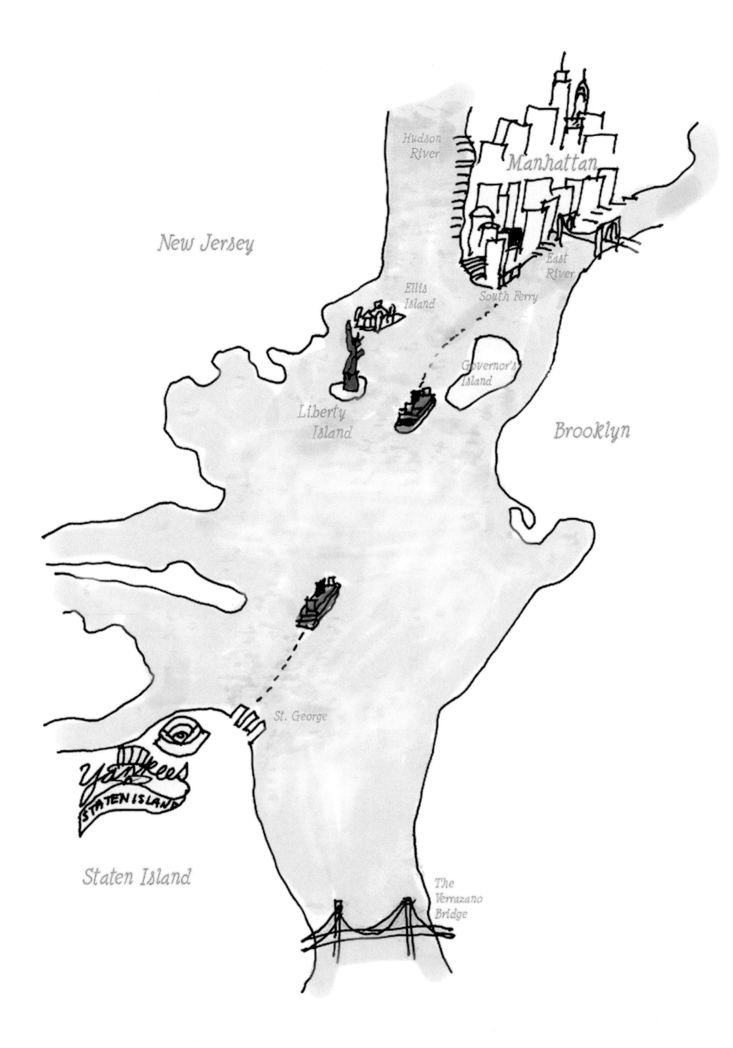

Today was going to be a very special day. Caleb was going to take the Staten Island Ferry to Manhattan. The Captain of the Ferry was Nick, who was also Caleb's grandfather. Captain Nick likes to take his grandson, Caleb with him on special days, and today was going to be very special.

The Ferries run 24 hours, seven days a week no matter what the weather is, except for hurricanes.

Today we are going on the American Legion. It was built in 1965. It is 277 feet long and can carry 3500 passengers, plus about 36 cars.

The crew on this ferry boat is:

Captain Nick,
the Assistant Captain,
the Mates,
and deckhands.
There is the Chief Marine Engineer,
who has a crew of one marine engineer and two marine oilersin the Engine Room that's below deck.

The doors of the terminal slide back and the boat begins to load. From the terminal two ramps lead the passengers onto the saloon deck.

Caleb is greeted by all the crew. They know he is Captain Nick's grandson. Caleb goes up to the Pilot House to see grandpa.

Captain Nick tells Caleb that this is going to be a special trip because the QE2 is leaving today to sail to England for the last time. He knows that Caleb's

favorite ocean liner is the QE2.

"Well then, let's get ready to sail," says Captain Nick, and asks Caleb to blow the ship's whistle.

This tells everyone the Ferry is leaving the dock, and the ferry is on time.

The view from the
Pilot House is awesome.
You can see the en-
tire harbor; from the

Verrazano Bridge, which is the
entrance to New York Harbor,
to the Statue of Liberty and
Ellis Island, and the skyline of
Manhattan with all its
bridges to Brooklyn and
Queens.

Today the weather is perfect. It is sunny with a few puffy white clouds and a light breeze that keeps the flags waving. Caleb is glad to share this day with his grandpa.

"Oh look, there is the QE2 coming down the Hudson River," John says. Captain Nick says: "I think we will meet her at the Statue of Liberty in about ten minutes."

Caleb then asks: "Grandpa, how many different boats do you see in a day?"

Nick answers: "Well, Caleb, in the summer you see the most. You have all the small boats; sailboats, cabin cruisers and jet skis then you have the yachts, cruise ships, container ships, bulk carriers, tankers, tugs, barges, fireboats, dredges, Coast Guard and Naval Ships, even Tall Ships.

The waterway is like a highway and there are rules that all Captains must follow.

There are certain places to anchor, like parking lots.

There are lanes you can go in and lanes to stay out of.

There are markers like street signs marking the way.

The buoys are different colors and different shapes.

Some mark the road others give information.

Nick then asked Caleb if he wanted to take the wheel while they sailed past the QE2.

"Wow, can I, grandpa?" Asked Caleb. With Nick on one side and the assistant captain on the other, Caleb grabbed the wheel.

The time was 5:07 P.M. the QE2 was just starting to pass the Statue of Liberty and the American Legion was also just passing the statue.

Slowly the statue disappeared behind the QE2. Caleb could not believe his eyes. He was steering the Staten Island Ferry past the QE2.

John, the deckhand always has a camera ready in his pocket, took a picture. John did not have to ask anyone to smile. Everyone was beaming.

Now they were passing Ellis Island. Nick was turning the ferry towards the East River. It's now 5:10 P.M.

Passing Ellis Island, Caleb tells the crew that his great-grandfather came to America as a teenager on a ship almost as big as the QE2. Caleb's great-grandfather was welcomed to America as an immigrant at Ellis Island.

Nick is doing a great job coming into the slip, not one bump on the sides of the slip.

The boat is tied to the dock and the ramps come down and let the passengers off.

Caleb gives his grandpa a big hug . Nick pats Caleb on the back and says: "It was a great trip and you will make a great captain someday. Tell your mother I'll be coming to dinner on Sunday."

Caleb thanks his grandfather and says: "Thanks for letting me steer the ferry. I know I'll always remember this as a special day."

The End

About the Author

Catherine Avery St. Jean grew up on the Mississippi River in Dubuque, Iowa. She is the oldest of eight kids (six brothers). She graduated from Loyola University in Chicago and then started a career in advertising.

She recently sold her company, Marcus St. Jean, an executive recruiting firm in Manhattan for advertising creative executives to go back to school and got her Masters Degree in Elementary Education.

In her spare time she also studies for her captains license. She lives on Staten Island.

About the Illustrator

Paul Frahm grew up in Portland, Oregon. He attended Stanford University and graduated from the University of Oregon, then studied at The Art Center School in California.

He got his start in advertising in San Francisco because he could draw storyboards. His 40 year career took him to New York, Paris and back to New York, working at several major ad agencies and winning many awards as an Art Director, TV Producer and Film Director.

He is still drawing and lives in Colorado.

Made in the USA
Middletown, DE
10 July 2023

34788078R10015